Suki Ferguson & Ana Novaes

YOUNG ORACLE TAROT

An initiation into tarot's mystic wisdom

WIDE EYED EDITIONS

Inspiring | Educating | Creating | Entertaining

Brimming with creative inspiration, how-to projects, and useful information to enrich your everyday life, Quarto Knows is a favorite destination for those pursuing their interests and passions. Visit our site and dig deeper with our books into your area of interest: Quarto Creates, Quarto Cooks, Quarto Homes, Quarto Lives, Quarto Drives, Quarto Explores, Quarto Gifts, or Quarto Kids.

Young Oracle Tarot © 2022 Quarto Publishing plc.
Text © 2022 Suki Ferguson. Illustrations © 2022 Ana Luiza de Novaes Campos.

First Published in 2022 by Wide Eyed Editions, an imprint of The Quarto Group.
100 Cummings Center, Suite 265D, Beverly, MA 01915, USA.
T +1 978-282-9590 F +1 078-283-2742 **www.QuartoKnows.com**

A CIP record for this book is available from the Library of Congress.

ISBN 978-0-71126-377-2

The illustrations were created using a mix of ink, watercolor, and digital techniques.
Set in Hustlers Rough, Appareo, Mac Magic Medieval, and Frosted
Published by Georgia Amson-Bradshaw
Edited by Hannah Dove
Designed by Sasha Moxon
Production by Dawn Cameron

Manufactured in Guangdong, China TT102021

9 8 7 6 5 4 3 2 1

MIX
Paper from responsible sources
FSC® C016973

CONTENTS

WELCOME, READER, TO THE WORLD OF TAROT

Mystery trails in the wake of these strange and beautiful cards. What are their origins? Are they safe, or sinister? And can they reveal the future?

For some, the cards inspire fear and suspicion. Yet rich rewards await those who approach tarot with openness and curiosity. Practice tarot from the heart, and you will deepen your inner strength, expand your self-knowledge, and better your connections with others.

Let's go on a journey through the tarot. In the coming pages, we will explore how tarot has evolved over the centuries from a medieval game to modern healing practice. Using the Rider-Waite-Smith deck, we will discover the meanings of each suit and each card. We will interpret symbols, learn ways to read the cards for ourselves and for others, and draw up wisdom from the deck.

Are you ready? Let us begin...

4

DEFINITIONS

Useful terms to refer to:

Arcane

Mysterious or secret; not understood by many.

Esoteric

As above; mysterious and little-known.

Iconography

The use of images and symbols to convey meanings.

Intuition

The ability to understand something through feeling rather than thinking.

Major Arcana

The twenty-two "trump cards" of the tarot deck, depicting significant life chapters.

Minor Arcana

The four suits of the tarot deck, depicting more fleeting experiences and feelings.

Occult

Relating to mystical powers or supernatural phenomena.

Oracle

In ancient times, oracles were priests or priestesses who could communicate with the spirit world, interpret mystic symbols, and guide truth-seekers in their decisions.

Querent

The person who seeks an answer from a tarot reading. This either refers to you in a reading, or to those you read for.

Spread

In tarot, a spread refers to the way the cards are arranged in a reading.

Unconscious

The part of our minds that affects our feelings and behavior without us realizing it.

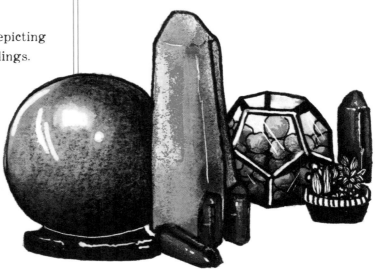

WHAT IS TAROT?

Tarot is a friend to all who know its secrets. Find out how a simple deck of cards can become your coach, your confidant, and your counsel.

Tarot cards are a special form of playing card. Unlike a usual deck of cards, they are not used to win at games. Instead, tarot cards exist to be interpreted. They are a tool that can help with solving problems and making decisions, by reflecting back conscious and unconscious thoughts and feelings—like a mirror. In this part of the book, we will explore how tarot works, trace its roots through time, and discover its modern uses.

HOW DOES TAROT WORK?

There is a very simple way to find out how tarot works. All you need is a single coin.

It can be any coin. Once you have found one, hold it in your hand and think of a yes/no question. It can be anything—*Do I want to see my friend tomorrow?* Heads means yes, tails means no. Focus on the question and flip the coin. The upward-facing side of the coin gives you your answer.

How do you feel? Maybe you feel disappointed in the coin's answer. Maybe you feel glad about it. Either way, the coin has answered your question.

The coin is just a coin. It doesn't know the workings of your mind, or your heart's desire.

Equally, what you do next is up to you—in this case, the coin is a prompt, not a command. But the simple act of flipping a coin has done something important. It has shown you how you feel.

Like the coin, tarot helps you conjure up your true feelings.

This is your intuition—the sum of your experiences, your sensations, your feelings. Your intuition is a powerful guide. You can access your intuition at any time and use it to test complex decisions. Sometimes a course of action looks appealing, or seems expected, but does it *feel* right, deep in your belly?

Intuition is at the heart of tarot. It may surprise you to learn that reading tarot cards won't predict your future or tell your fortune. But it will help you uncover your unconscious feelings and gut instincts.

You ask the cards questions. The cards show you possibilities. Your intuition gives you an answer. However, unlike a simple coin, where only two replies are possible, a single tarot card will contain layered and multiple meanings. Each card contains symbols, numbers, colors, and images that can be explored.

Understanding these layers is an evolving process—there is the commonly accepted meaning of the card, and then there is the personal interpretation that you develop, using that information and your own experiences.

How you read the cards will also evolve over time—even within the span of a few days, your feelings toward a particular card can shift dramatically as your circumstances change.

We come to tarot with questions. But the question that matters most is the one asked by the cards: *how does this make you feel?*

TAROT THROUGH TIME

Though its recorded history is patchy, tarot is traceable through the centuries. Its evolution is fascinating, from being an exclusive amusement for aristocrats, to a tool for self-exploration, loved by people around the world. And this evolution continues—we can only imagine how it may be used in the future!

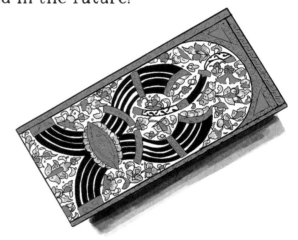

1300s North Africa & Turkey

Intricately designed cards featuring suits of Coins, Goblets, Swords, and Polo-Sticks emerge within the North African Islamic Mamluk empire. These cards gradually reach Italy and the rest of Europe.

800s China

Records show that woodblock-printed cards are used for playing games. Through the coming centuries, more and more cards are printed and they travel west across India, the Middle East, and beyond.

1463 Italy

A wealthy Italian nobleman commissions an artist to create twenty-two cards. They feature concepts, such as The Fool and The World. These cards, known as the Visconti-Sforza, make up the first recorded tarot deck.

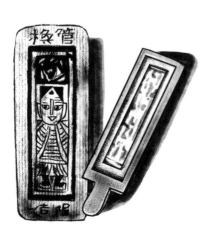

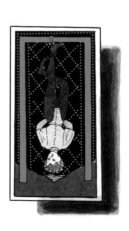

1650 France

The Tarot de Marseilles is created in France. Featuring bright illustrations that are easily replicated using woodcut printing, this deck becomes popular with occultists.

1785 France

The first professional tarot reader, a French man known as Etteila, popularizes tarot as a tool for fortune-telling by writing a guide to using the cards.

1480s Europe

Playing cards, featuring what we now know as Clubs, Diamonds, Hearts, and Spades, are created in France for mass use. Wealthy Italian families continue to commission bespoke tarot decks decorated with gold for use as a parlour game, to prompt poetry, and for amusement, and self-knowledge.

1781 France

An occultist named Antoine Court de Gébelin writes about tarot, claiming that it has mystical, Ancient Egyptian origins. This theory catches on within British and French occult circles, and tarot's mysterious reputation grows.

11

1800s England

Victorian society experiences a craze for all things supernatural and mystical. Seances (meetings where people try to talk with dead spirits), magic shows, fortune-telling, and tarot readings are popular activities.

Whole nations are engulfed in the violence of the two World Wars. Tarot fades from the public eye.

1910 England

The Rider-Waite-Smith tarot deck is first published and becomes the new standard for tarot.

1960s–1970s

Tarot regains popularity within Western countercultural movements that reject greed and violence. Instead of fortune-telling and mysticism, the cards are used for guidance and self-discovery.

2010–2020

Social media makes it easier to learn about tarot. Artists from around the world create decks that depict queer identities, racial identities, and indigenous cultures. Tarot reaches more people than ever before, and is practiced as a form of care, guidance, and reflection.

1980s–2000s

Western artists create tarot decks that reflect the importance of feminism, goddess worship, and nature worship. Tarot becomes popular in Japan, where artists make anime and manga versions, and in India, where tarot is a hit with marriage matchmakers.

Tarot Today

Tarot has become more and more accessible over the centuries. Until recently, it could be hard to know where to start. Learning about tarot depended on who you knew, where you lived, and what circles you moved in. Now, thanks to the internet, anyone can purchase a deck online, and learn about card meanings and spreads there too. Tarot readers today can tap into the wisdom and creativity of a global tarot community, in a way that would not have been possible in the past.

Take a look at just a tiny selection of the hundreds of tarot decks now available to the modern tarot practitioner.

The Modern Witch Tarot

An inclusive deck that brings the Rider-Waite-Smith deck up-to-date for modern practitioners.

The Wild Unknown Tarot

A darkly evocative modern deck featuring wild animals with mythic associations.

The Goddess Tarot

A deck that features the sacred women of many belief systems from around the world.

The Neo Tarot

A bright and stylish deck that remixes the Rider-Waite-Smith design with a queer-friendly, body-positive approach.

Or simply make your own cards! Fill a sketchbook with your ideal versions of the Major Arcana. Make a deck that matches up to the world you dream of—and use it. Let your own visions shape how you use and interpret the tarot. Your creativity makes you part of a centuries-old tradition of reinventing these magical cards.

DISCOVERING THE DECKS

In the past, it would have been quite difficult to come across tarot cards, or arrange to have your cards read. Today, there are thousands of tarot decks available and tarot readers can choose cards that celebrate every aspect of existence.

This book teaches from the Rider-Waite-Smith deck. Created in 1910, this deck's widespread availability and symbolism has made it a go-to beginner's deck. It is also the most reinvented one—with most modern decks using it as a template. Being able to confidently interpret the Rider-Waite-Smith deck enables you to read almost any modern tarot deck.

Like all older tarot decks, however, the cards present a limited and narrow version of human experience. For example, the Rider-Waite-Smith features only white people, and the symbols draw mostly on Christianity and Judaism, or Ancient Greek and Roman myths. The gender roles shown in cards such as The Emperor and The Lovers replicate out-of-date ideas about power and love.

Modern decks are much more inclusive and representative of society, and draw on a much wider range of faiths, cultures, myths, and ideals. So, while knowing the Rider-Waite-Smith deck is great for getting to grips with tarot, don't be afraid to venture beyond it. Seek out a deck that speaks to you!

Pamela Colman Smith

The illustrations of the Rider-Waite-Smith deck are recognizable the world over and have become synonymous with tarot, with images like The Sun cropping up in pop culture, from films to fashion.

The artist behind these illustrations was Pamela Colman Smith. Called Pixie by her friends, she was once described as "goddaughter of a witch and sister to a fairy!" She was born in 1878 in England to American parents. As a teenager, Pixie lived in Jamaica and New York. At the age of twenty-one she settled in London and worked as a theater-maker, folk storyteller, and illustrator.

A friend to leading suffragettes, Pixie designed women's suffrage movement posters for free, and published stories by women writers at a time when such a thing was very subversive. Pixie created art for all seventy-eight cards of the 1910 Rider-Waite-Smith deck, which became an enduring success.

Despite the popularity of the Rider-Waite -Smith deck, the publishers paid Pixie very little for her work, and in time her style fell out of fashion. Long after her death, in the 1970s, a new generation of tarot lovers rediscovered Pixie's work, and today she is celebrated as an inspired illustrator whose talent helped bring tarot to the world.

TAROT AS A TOOL

Practicing tarot is an art and a skill. Learn it and you can use it to look after your mental health, help others, develop your power to make change, and simply have a good time.

☾ Tarot & play

Before anything else, tarot was invented as a game to be played among friends! The beauty of the cards gives us a thrill—and they allow us to whisper our secrets, revel in new possibilities, and laugh at the dramas of our lives.

✳ Tarot & decision-making

If you are unsure of yourself or feeling stuck, a three-card reading (problem–cause–solution) can quickly bring you clarity (see page 77). Even a single-card reading will cast new light on an otherwise baffling situation (see page 76). Tarot enables you to acknowledge your dilemma and consider the options open to you. Next time you feel uncertain about a choice you're facing, your deck can help you tap into your intuition and work it out.

16

✳ Tarot & mental well-being

At times, life can be a real drag. Things that used to be fun become dull. Family and friends do upsetting things. We even disappoint ourselves. In moments of crisis or sadness, tarot is there for you, no matter what. All you need is the cards. Working with them allows you to work through your feelings, and find comfort. And by giving caring and confidential readings to friends, you can offer that comfort when they are having a hard time, too.

☀ Tarot & activism

Humanity today faces many problems, including lack of care for others, lack of care for the natural world, and greed. These global problems can also exist at a small scale in our own lives. But before we can change anything, we must first connect with our own power.

Tarot helps us recognize our flaws and strengths. It can also help us see how we respond to challenges. Do we rage, or run, or give up? When we understand ourselves, we are better-equipped to use our power well and meet problems head-on, with creativity and joy.

Next time you confront a knotty issue that requires action, such as shifting outdated attitudes, or changing how we use resources, try consulting the cards. Ask "what can I do here?" and tarot can help you come up with an approach that feels right to you.

ABOUT THE CARDS

Getting to know a tarot deck is an exciting process. Across the seventy-eight cards, there are symbols, colors, and moods, all jostling for attention. In this section, you can take time getting to know the cards and their meanings.

Befriend your cards! Keep them in a special box or
wrapped in a piece of silk. Treated with care, they will
serve you for a long time, and be there for you in moments
of curiosity, self-doubt, confusion, and anticipation.

WITHIN THE DECK

Discover the different parts of a typical tarot deck

Major Arcana

The first twenty-two cards of a tarot deck are unique to tarot. Called the Major Arcana, and numbered from zero to twenty-one, these cards look mysterious, and are loaded with meaning. Each card in the Major Arcana represents a major chapter in life—though how you feel about each card may change as often as your circumstances do!

The Major Arcana cards show us emotions and experiences that can shape our lives: grief, hope, joy, confusion, fear, love, and more.

They also show us figures who embody powerful roles that are likely to influence us, such as mother (The Empress), father (The Emperor), and teacher (The Hierophant).

THE EMPRESS.

THE EMPEROR.

THE HIEROPHANT.

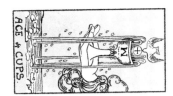

✺ Minor Arcana

The Minor Arcana is the name for the cards in a tarot deck outside of the Major Arcana. There are fifty-six cards in the Minor Arcana, divided across four suits, and they depict a wide array of experience and feelings.

In a reading, the cards of the Minor Arcana can be as influential as those of the Major Arcana, but are tied to more specific circumstances—such as work or learning. The cards of the Minor Arcana describe the passing moods and smaller shifts of our lives.

✳ The Four Suits

The Minor Arcana is made up of four suits, like a pack of playing cards. Like playing cards, each of the four suits has an Ace, a Queen, and a King. In the tarot, each suit has a Knight instead of a Jack, and a fourth court card, featuring a youthful Page. In a reading, the Page, Knight, Queen, and King cards often represent people in our lives.

Each of the four tarot suits represents a different focus. The Swords (pp.54–61) represent thought, reason, and decision-making. Air is the Swords' element. The Pentacles (pp.62–69)—sometimes known as Coins—explore security, wealth, and practicality. Their associated element is the earth. The Cups (pp.38–45) represent intuition, emotion, and fluidity, and their element is water. Fire belongs to the Wands suit (pp.46–53), which refers to projects, energy, and work.

SYMBOLS & MEANINGS

Tarot cards are packed with visual clues. Interpreting a tarot card can be like working out a puzzle, and each deck contains its own symbols to be decoded. Here, we look at a selection of symbols that crop up in the Rider-Waite-Smith deck. When looking at your cards, what other symbols can you identify?

Water

Water is ever-changing—sometimes still, sometimes swirling. It nourishes life, and yet is essentially wild. Water symbolizes emotions. It appears in many guises in tarot—in rain, pools, rivers, and seas—and is often paired with Cups.

Birds

In folklore around the world, birds are seen as messengers of the gods. In tarot they symbolize divinity, yet different birds have subtly different meanings. In The Star, an ibis—bird of the Ancient Egyptian god Thoth—suggests rebirth and insight. In the Ace of Cups, a white dove, associated with peace, blesses the image. And the Swords suit features birds in flight: a symbol of freedom.

Butterflies

Butterflies are creatures of the air, and in the Rider-Waite-Smith deck, they are found in the Swords suit. They symbolize transformation: moving from caterpillar to chrysalis to butterfly, they are not able to fly at every stage of their life—but it is their destiny to do so.

22

✴ Dwellings

Whether grand or humble, the cottages, villages, and castles of the Rider-Waite-Smith deck represent home and community; a destination for the traveler, and a place for friendship, family, and routine life. A dwelling invites the querent to ask: *What does community mean to me right now?*

◖ Mountains

Mountains symbolize struggle and aspiration, because climbing a mountain involves challenge, risk, and determination. The presence of mountains on a card can also indicate a call to leave everyday concerns behind, and be closer to the spiritual side of life.

✴ Weather & time of day

Do you see calm seas or storm clouds? Dawning light or gathering gloom? We are affected by weather—we hunch against cold winds, and sweat beneath the sun. Tarot illustrations draw on this power.

☀ Colors

Most tarot decks use color to amplify the meaning of a card. In the Rider-Waite-Smith deck, bright, warm colors appear on cards associated with contentment, comfort, and wealth. Cool-toned cards convey more solemn messages. At the end of a reading, look at all the colors—a spread filled with yellows and neutrals indicates encouragement. A spread filled with darker shades may reflect a more troubled situation.

☽ Body language

If a card features a person, or several people, you can learn a lot by looking at body language. Do they look outward, and meet your gaze—and if so, do they look happy, kindly, or stern? Or do they look away, and maybe even hide their face? Perhaps they are engrossed in something—perhaps that is where our attention should go, too.

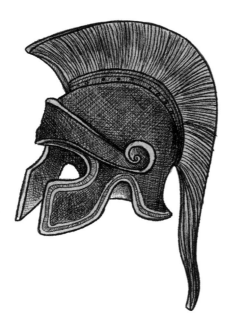

✳ Clothing

How a person is dressed in the tarot is never an accident. If they are wearing armor, this symbolizes being ready for battle; if they are naked, this symbolizes vulnerability, and an openness to what the world may bring. Flowing robes suggest comfort and happiness. Torn rags indicate adversity. If you see patterns on clothes, look closely—they may contain symbols that deepen your interpretation.

☉ Scale, size, & detail

In some cards, the focal point is large, obvious, and unavoidable. In others, many people or symbols crowd the scene. Does the image feel intense, or gentle and meandering? The scale and size of a card's features can be a good thing to check. How do you feel about the simplicity or complexity of the image?

When a card is upside down, this is called a reversed card. In a reading, this means that the energy of the card is blocked or flipped in some way.

If you draw The Sun, for example, and it is reversed, this suggests that you may be feeling listless, tired, or insecure. Or perhaps you pull the Ten of Swords and it is reversed—this would suggest that there is a serious issue that you haven't considered, and need to explore and let go of in order to proceed.

Card reversals can be something you use to bring a new layer of meaning into your readings. To shuffle your deck in a way that produces reversed cards, just spread out all your cards in a big heap, face down, and swirl them around with your hands. Mix them up and around, and then bring them back into a neat stack. When you pull cards for a reading, some will be reversed.

Not every tarot card reader uses reversals, but many do. Experiment with reversals and see how it develops your readings.

THE MAJOR ARCANA

The Major Arcana are a series of twenty-two cards that are seen as the foundation of the tarot deck. Each card represents major chapters in a person's life. In a reading, if you draw one of the Major Arcana cards, give the card special weight in your interpretation. If several Major Arcana cards show up in your reading, step back and look at your life as a whole. What big shifts may be at work?

Draw the Major Arcana cards from the pack and lay them out in order, starting at zero (The Fool) and ending with twenty-one (The World). Arrange them in a line and see what feelings the images prompt in you.

The Major Arcana cards tell a story—the story of the Fool's Journey. The Fool's Journey can be best understood when we arrange the cards in a circle, starting with zero at the top, and moving clockwise and around to number twenty-one. If we journey around the circle as The Fool, we move from learning the rules and seeking guidance and wisdom, to experiencing setbacks, experiencing happiness, and finally coming to a place of belonging.

We go through our lives in phases, and each phase has the power to teach us and change us. The true nature of life can be seen when we lay out the Major Arcana as a circle. All being well, we will go on The Fool's journey many times in our lives.

o. The Fool

ı. The Magician

THE FOOL.

THE MAGICIAN.

eginnings 🌙 *innocence*
✴ *trust*

power ✳ *ability*
☀ *readiness*

The Fool is about being carefree and vulnerable. A young person walks through a wilderness, gazing at the sky. They are not well-equipped for a difficult journey, carrying only a few possessions, with a playful pet dog at their side. Their next step may even lead them over a precipice—if so, will they recover? Still, the sun shines upon them, and they have faith in the path they walk upon. This card is about feeling excited about the world and setting off on an unpredictable journey. You are trying something new, despite the risks, and just for the fun of it.

The Magician stands at a table laid with a cup, a sword, a wand, and a pentacle. These represent the suits in the tarot, and all of their symbolic powers: feeling, thought, action, and practicality. He has every tool that he needs within reach. Still, he does not rush to use them—he will act when the time is right. In a reading, this card invites you to take note of the things you are good at—and not just academic stuff. The Magician calls on you to practice your skills. Develop them, and learn wisdom as you use them to achieve your goals. Which tools lie on your table?

THE HIGH PRIESTESS.

2. The High Priestess

mystery 🌙 *insight*
✴ *intuition*

The High Priestess is an oracle and a seer, guarding the underworld. Like the moon, the tides, and the seasons, she symbolizes the changeable aspect of nature, and of ourselves. Sometimes we shine, sometimes we fade. She represents silence, stillness, and the mysterious power of our unconscious. In a reading, this card suggests that peace and quiet will help you tune in to your inner wisdom. If you sit for a while, breathe deeply, and reflect upon your dilemmas, what new insights emerge?

3. The Empress

pleasure ✴ *joy*
☀ *life-giving*

The Empress is surrounded by a golden harvest, sitting upon a throne inscribed with the symbol of Venus, the Greek goddess of love. She is affectionate, experiencing life through her senses as well as her mind. If you met the Empress, she would be sure to give you a warm hug. In loving her own life, she is able to love others. She can bring motherly energy into a reading. The Empress reminds us that we are part of the wonder of nature, we are loveable and we are more than enough—we are bountiful and capable of joy.

THE EMPRESS.

THE EMPEROR.

The Emperor sits squarely on a [...] carved with horned rams, wearing [...] swathed in royal robes. He represen[ts...] ability to govern ourselves and take c[...] Can we resist temptations and do [...] properly, even when that isn't easy? Car[...] disciplined and make good on what we s[...] to achieve? In a reading, this card invit[es...] to conjure up a stern yet fatherly figur[e...] Emperor reminds us that playing by th[e...] can bring peace of mind and rich rewar[ds...]

5. The Hierophant

teaching ✳ *learning*
☀ *conforming*

The word "hierophant" means "displayer of holy things" in Greek. Here, the Hierophant sits on a throne much like the High Priestess and the Emperor. Like them, he is powerful. His power is less about mystery or control, though; he is a teacher who attracts followers eager to defer to his wisdom. Two such followers sit at his feet. The Hierophant is about seeking knowledge through things like school, or a religious text. This card suggests that there is value in convention—the teacher speaks so that the pupil may learn.

THE HIEROPHANT.

6. The Lovers

THE LOVERS.

real love 🌓 *equality*
✴ *unity*

The Lovers are naked, blessed by an angel and the sun above. This deck shows them as a woman and a man, but more and more, modern tarot decks are offering interpretations of The Lovers that recognize and celebrate queer love. The presence of The Lovers in a reading can refer to romantic love. It can also mean finding joy in another person or uniting with someone despite your differences. To find harmony in a relationship, each person must truly value the other. Love is not a one-sided thing; this card reminds us to value love that goes both ways.

7. The Chariot

THE CHARIOT.

determination ✴
persistence ☀ *beginning*

The charioteer, dressed for battle, stands firmly in the block of a chariot pulled by two sphinxes, one black, one white. He is ready to take on what the world throws at him, uniting opposing forces whilst driving forward with great confidence. The Chariot invites you to use willpower to reach your goals. It's time to recognize your strengths, set aside your doubts and accept that things won't be easy. Then grit your teeth—and begin! Take a steady approach to overcome obstacles, and stay the course.

8. Strength

STRENGTH.

urage ☾ *self-knowledge*
✴ *influence*

A figure bends over a lion, calmly drawing its head into their hands. This is not about physical force or a battle of wills. This card celebrates something that may not be obvious at first glance: inner strength. Take a look at your deepest fears and embarrassments—and then be kind to yourself about them. In its fullest role, Strength is about harnessing our animal fears and desires, then expressing them without shame. This kind of strength enables others to be free to express themselves, too.

9. The Hermit

THE HERMIT.

retreat ✴ *inner visior*
◉ *solitude*

The Hermit stands in an icy lands holding a bright lantern to ligh way—yet his eyes are closed, and still. He symbolizes the wisdom of tu inward; he invites us to choose solitu order to see clearly. When you are al around other people, always busy, it too easy to forget about things that m to *you*. The Hermit may be alone, b is not lonely. In this way he differs similar-looking cards, such as the Fi Cups, where solitude is a source of pai

10. Wheel of Fortune

luck ☾ *opportunities* ✳ *fate*

WHEEL of FORTUNE.

This card is full of intriguing symbols, but its message is simple: chance can transform our lives for the better. The world never stops changing, and we all experience those rare moments of being in the right place at the right time. You can't plan for these moments, but you can be attentive to them, and be ready for them. Equally, sometimes fate goes against us, and what will be will be. The Wheel of Fortune invites us to respect the greater powers that shape our lives, and be open to whatever may come.

11. Justice

fairness ✳ *decision-making* ☀ *responsibility*

Justice holds up a sword, symbolizing reason, and scales for weighing up opposing elements. With her direct gaze and imposing surroundings, The Justice card is all about taking responsibility. This can mean taking an upcoming decision seriously or taking care to be fairer to others. It can also be a reminder to accept the consequences that arise from our actions. Justice asks, are you being your best self? Are you making the right choices? In a reading, this card says that being truthful and self-aware will serve you well.

JUSTICE.

The Hanged Man

The Hanged Man

surrender ✳ *patience*
☽ *serenity*

The Hanged Man shows us a peaceful-looking person, suspended upside-down from a cross. The figure bears a halo, suggesting enlightenment. The Hanged Man is about letting things be. Sometimes it is right to do everything in your power to change things. At other times, it is better to stop struggling, and just let go. Choosing to accept an imperfect new situation, or to give up something you care about, can set you free. By taking this patient approach, you may find that you begin to see things in a new light.

THE HANGED MAN.

DEATH.

13. Death

change ◉ *endings*
✳ *acceptance*

A skeleton rides a pale horse, b a victory banner. All fall benea horse's hooves. When the Death card co in your reading, it is rarely about death it is there to remind us that all things eve come to an end. Maybe a friendship, love or a chapter in your life is ending. Th affirms the pain that arises when this ha We cope with loss best when we let ou feel it and remember that something ne arise. Look to the sun, rising on the horizon bringing a new day.

14. Temperance

TEMPERANCE.

health 🌙 *balance*
✳ *moderation*

An angel pours water back and forth between two cups. One foot is in a pool of water, symbolizing emotions; the other is on firm ground, symbolizing practical needs. Temperance invites us to seek a happy balance in our lives. Recall a time when you felt full of well-being. Perhaps you got plenty of sleep, plenty of food to eat, and all was well for you and those you care about. There are no extremes here—Temperance is all about valuing the gentle things that sustain us.

15. The Devil

THE DEVIL.

craving ✳ *weakness*
☀ *isolation*

The Devil crouches above two figures— perhaps The Lovers—who are in chains, and subject to his will. In the tarot, The Devil is about feeling powerless. Maybe you've been feeling pressure to fit in and betraying your true values. Maybe you've been chasing short-term highs and now feel empty. Maybe you are putting energy into shallow things. Whatever is preoccupying you leaves you feeling bad. This card is here to say that what you are experiencing is part of being human. Recognizing that there is an issue will enable you to make changes.

16. The Tower

17. The Star

XVI

THE TOWER.

XVII

THE STAR.

destruction ☾ *shock*
✴ *change*

hope ✳ *reassurance*
☀ *renewal*

The Tower shows a fortress being struck by lightning. Crowned figures fall from the castle walls. Here, The Tower symbolizes certainty: the way we tend to assume that things will always be as they seem. The bolt of lightning strikes and shakes the tower, reminding us that nothing is certain, and we are works in progress. A statement like "I am good at science, but I'm not funny" may *feel* true—but may not always be so. A shock can quickly upend old assumptions. This card prompts you to explore new aspects of yourself, and reveal unexpected possibilities.

The figure in this card pours water onto the earth and into a lake. Stars blaze in the clear skies above her, and she is completely at ease in her body. When you are weary, sad, and at a low ebb, The Star card brings you solace and says, "you are okay." In a reading, this card invites you to connect with things that inspire hope in you. When you feel dull and fed up, do a little of what you love—it will help you revive your sparkle. Think of it like water, springing up through the earth, bringing life back to the land, and back to you.

18. The Moon

confusion  *imagination* ✦ *self-deception*

Night comes and makes our world strange to us. A dog and a wolf yowl at the moon. A crayfish leaves its watery home. This card conjures the shadowy, chaotic side of our imaginations. Sometimes we lose sleep worrying about things that will never happen, or wake up from nightmares that feel very real. Sometimes we feed our fears, by keeping them secret, or even by chasing thrills. The Moon card reminds us that though our anxieties can have an irresistible quality, we feel better when we focus on our dreams and goals.

THE MOON.

19. The Sun

confidence ✦ *happiness* ✦ *success*

The Sun beams down on a row of sunflowers and a horse with a young child on its back. The child radiates delight: there is no reserve in the way they embrace life. This card speaks to feeling true confidence. There are times in our lives when everything goes right. All confusion and fear drops away, and we are able to be everything we hope to be. In these moments, we shine. The Sun card invites you to revel in your vitality, believe in your abilities, and trust the blessings that come to you.

JUDGEMENT.

20. Judgement

decision-making ✷
forgiveness ☾ *rebirth*

The call of an angel awakens people from a death-like state.. They look up in awe. Judgement is a card steeped in Christian imagery relating to Judgement Day and the Resurrection. In a reading, Judgement can be about making an important decision. When you feel called to take a particular course, trust that feeling! Your sense of purpose will help you rise to the occasion. Judgement can also suggest setting things right. If you have hurt someone's feelings, instead of defending your actions, make amends. Accountability and forgiveness renew us, and bring a sense of freedom.

21. The World

wholeness ☀ *contentment*
✷ *giving back*

A woman dances in the air, at one with the universe. The World is the card that means fulfillment. You feel blissful because you belong. You have overcome a great deal to reach this state of being, and the journey has helped you see that you are blessed. This card invites you to savor the present, treasure moments of harmony, and share your gifts. Enjoy your accomplishments; be playful and inventive with them; use them to help others. The world needs you, and you need the world. By being here, you make the world a better place.

THE WORLD.

THE CUPS

The Cups suit is all about feelings and intuitions. These cards help us to explore the depth of our emotions and how we handle them. They ask us if we are attuned to how we feel, and how others feel. The Cups suit also mirrors our spiritual side—the side of us that feels the wonder and mystery of being alive.

Symbolism

Cups cards often feature images of water. In the tarot, water symbolizes emotion. This is because water is changeable, unpredictable, and nourishing, just like emotions. Cups are vessels, made to hold these water-emotions. When a cup stands upright, it suggests that your feelings are in a good place. When a cup is lying on its side, it suggests that a good feeling has been lost. Water is meaningful elsewhere in the Cups cards: a river, like the one in the Five of Cups, symbolizes sorrow. Water touching a person in your card, as in the Queen of Cups, suggests being in touch with your feelings.

Drawing up the Cups

Draw all of the Cups cards from your deck and line them up from Ace to King. What feelings do these particular cards prompt in you? The Cups suit contains many moments of joy, and some moments of loss, too.

Ace of Cups

ACE of CUPS.

expressing emotion 🌙
empathy ✳ *new love*

Acup overflows, blessed by a dove, which symbolizes peace. This is a card that invites us to get in touch with our feelings and express ourselves, perhaps in a creative way. A card for beginnings, in the Cups suit the Ace may mean that a seed of love is present in your life. Perhaps a new friendship or romance will soon bloom. The Ace of Cups also reminds us that true intimacy—being close to someone—develops best when we are loving, curious, and trusting with each other.

Two of Cups

cooperation ✳
reconciliation ◉ *attraction*

Two people face each other, and each holds a cup. They are a well-matched pair, dressed in fine clothes, and almost mirroring each other's postures. The Two of Cups shows us a partnership, where two people are closely connected. They could be in love; they could be working together; they could be friends. In a reading, they can symbolize making peace after an argument, and finding a way to agree. The Two of Cups can also invite you to acknowledge a growing attraction. Is there someone you want to be close to?

Three of Cups

friendship ☾ fun ☀ community

Three women raise three chalices in a celebratory toast. A ripe harvest surrounds them and, in many decks, they dance together in a circle. The Three of Cups celebrates good times and high spirits. It reminds us that finding our soulmates—the friends who really "get" you—is not just enjoyable, it is life-giving! In a reading, this card may be an invitation to reach out to people who care about the same things that you care about. When you do find others who are on your wavelength, be sure to cherish them.

Four of Cups

withdrawing ✳ boredom ☀ shutting down

A young person sits beneath a tree, absorbed in contemplation. They do not seem to notice the cup being offered to them. The Four of Cups suggests that you have reached a point where you feel a bit stuck, and you are starting to seek inspiration—but you are not quite ready to receive it. This card recognizes that we all feel bored or overwhelmed sometimes, and that it's okay to let new opportunities pass you by occasionally. We can't be open to every possibility at all times.

Five of Cups

disappointment ✳
loneliness ☾ *hope*

The hunched figure in the Five of Cups stands alone, enveloped in a black cloak. Their gaze is fixed upon three knocked-over cups. This card speaks to feeling upset over a failure or loss that is hard to move on from. The upset may be over, but you still feel disappointed and lonely. If you look around, however, the picture brightens. Two upright cups behind the figure symbolize happier feelings waiting to be seen. Though a river seems to separate the figure from a distant town, they can cross a bridge to reach it. This card reminds you that you will find company and comfort, when you seek it.

Six of Cups

happiness ☉ *looking back*
✳ *innocence*

The Six of Cups features children using a cup to gather flowers and enjoy their scent. They play in a courtyard, protected from the world. This is a card that invites us to revisit joyous experiences in our minds, particularly after enduring a difficult time. Sometimes when we are stressed or struggling, we can forget what it feels like to be playful, curious and feel wonder at the beauty of the world. Happy memories remind us of our ability to enjoy life. The Six of Cups suggests that these memories can point the way back to feeling good again.

Seven of Cups

imagination ☽ *fantasy*
✷ *distraction.*

A figure is transfixed by cups that dance in the air, each seeming to promise wild gifts and strange visions, from jewels and castles to ghosts and dragons. This card is all about daydreams: letting our minds run free is liberating and can show us new worlds. Just by following our imaginations we can make anything happen—in our heads. But making things happen in reality is difficult, and not every daydream can come true. When this card emerges, take a moment to sort your goals from your fantasies.

Eight of Cups

leaving ✳ *withdrawing*
☀ *moving on*

A person walks away from rows of upright cups and retreats into a rocky, moonlit landscape, alone. Their journey feels deliberate: they walk with a staff, similar to The Hermit. This card invites us to step away from the sociable aspect of the Cups suit and seek deeper self-knowledge for a while. Perhaps you are thinking of leaving a friendship group, or a team of some kind. It's okay to leave the hubbub behind and seek space to rest and reflect. Use your alone time to make sense of what your experiences

Nine of Cups

IX

satisfaction ☾ *relaxing*
✴ *enjoying luxury*

The Nine of Cups shows a contented man, surrounded by his cups. He is richly dressed and wears a smile. Maybe he has enjoyed a feast, or won a prize, or heard good news. Perhaps all three happened at once! In a reading, this card invites you to take pleasure in your successes. There is a warning here, too: being smug or showing off can be hurtful to those who are struggling. But the Nine of Cups still urges you to indulge in your happiness, when it comes. Protect it, and savor it!

Ten of Cups

X

delight ✴ *togetherness*
◉ *family*

A glorious rainbow arcs above a family and a green land. The two children play, delighting in the moment, while the parents hold each other and rejoice in the scene before them. This is one of the most radiant cards in the tarot, and it reminds us to appreciate sweet moments and joyous family occasions. When things are really good, we notice that we feel full-hearted and at peace. We become able to get over our differences, forgive each other for past errors, and treasure ordinary family bonds.

PAGE of CUPS.

Page of Cups

imagination  *trust*
learning

In every suit, the Page represents learning—in the Cups suit, he eagerly seeks to understand his emotions. And there is much to understand: to start with, what's that fish doing in his cup?! Here it represents the unfamiliar: new opportunities and new feelings. The Page of Cups responds with a playful curiosity. In a reading, this card might refer to a young person, or someone with a trusting nature. They could be a friend, a sibling, an admirer, or someone who *you* admire. The Page of Cups invites you to channel their open nature and welcome fresh experiences.

Knight of Cups

sensitivity ✴ *self-*
expression ☀ *unreliability.*

Each Knight reveals the extremes of his suit. In the Cups suit, the Knight is a true romantic, led by his heart. He is attuned to his feelings—yet his sensitivity can make him touchy. He is attractive and imaginative—but quick to feel disappointed by real life. At a party, he would notice if you were feeling awkward and set you at ease, but he wouldn't think to clear up once the fun was over. In a reading, this card can represent someone you like, or it can reflect your own habits and remind you that it is good to balance your head and your heart.

KNIGHT of CUPS.

Queen of Cups

emotional intelligence ✴
creativity ☾ *compassion*

This contemplative Queen is at ease around swirling waters. She understands emotions on an almost psychic level, and feels great pain and joy, in others as well as in herself. She is creative, loving all artistic modes of self-expression. For her, nature is sacred, and she feels deeply for all living things. She listens to people and is skilled at meeting their anger and despair with love. In a reading, she may refer to someone in your life, or she may inspire you to follow her path of empathy.

QUEEN of CUPS.

KING of CUPS.

King of Cups

diplomatic ☀ *warm*
✴ *cultured*

The King of Cups is a kind soul who can settle even the most bitter of disputes with his even-handed insight. You can turn to the King of Cups for good advice. He is friends with people from all backgrounds, and appreciates artistry in all its forms, seeking out and finding meaning in creative endeavors. He is open-minded, aware of his emotions, and feels no shame in expressing them. In a reading, he may serve as a role model for you to emulate or remind you of a similar person in your life.

THE WANDS

The Wands suit is all about energy! These cards help us to explore our capabilities and creativity. What sparks your interest? Which activities fuel your inner fire? The Wands represent work, play, and inspiration, bringing focus and vitality to the tarot deck.

Symbolism

The Wands cards are linked with fire—the golden robes of the King, Knight, and Page of Wands all depict the salamander, which, according to myth, can walk through flames unscathed. In the tarot, fire represents energy. Like fire, energy sustains us but it can also flicker out, or run riot. When interpreting a Wands card, it helps to see each wand as a project, task, or goal: if the person on your card holds only one wand, you may be in need of a challenge. If they hold ten wands, you may be overwhelmed.

The wands themselves also represent growth. Leaves sprout on them, and they have ancient symbolic associations with fertility. Of all the suits, the Wands refer to our creative ability the most. We can all do and make in our own individual ways. These cards encourage you to follow your passion and go about your activities wholeheartedly.

Drawing up the Wands

Draw all of the Wands cards from your deck and line them up from Ace to King. What feelings do these particular cards prompt in you? The Wands suit contains many moments of action, and struggles too.

ACE of WANDS.

energy ☾ *boldness*
✳ *readiness*

self-assurance ✴ *powe*
◉ *purpose*

The Wands represent action, and drawing the Ace of Wands is like being given a surge of pure energy. Here you can see that the wand itself is a living thing, budding with green leaves; seize it like the hand in the card is your own! Embrace growth and life's incredible possibilities. You may have cause to hesitate, but this is a trump card: it says, "Get started—now is the time to make things happen." This card invites you to rise to a new challenge with confidence.

A regal figure holds the worl one hand, a wand in the other, gazes out to sea. Great things have b accomplished—this is someone who kn his power and what he can do with it may even be bored, and in search of f challenges that will test him. In a read the Two of Wands invites you to assured. You've done well—take a around and enjoy the view. It also call you to be inventive and apply yourse any fresh problems in your life. Let t

Three of Wands

vision *exploration*
 leadership

A figure looks out on a stretch of sea where ships sail. Beneath their robes they wear armor—they are ready to take risks. The two wands behind the figure suggest further, unseen, opportunities that have yet to be grasped. The Three of Wands suggests being prepared in a practical sense, but also having vision. What is coming? In a reading, this card encourages you to move out of your comfort zone and seek new adventures. The Three of Wands reminds you that being ready to try something new often results in exciting discoveries.

Four of Wands

celebration *community*
 delight

A celebration is underway beyond the confines of the city walls. It could be seasonal or ceremonial; the mood is light and fun-filled. Garlands of flowers decorate the space. This card evokes festivals, parties, weddings, holidays, and family feasts—special occasions where people get together for happy reasons and gather as a temporary community outside the routines of daily life. Freedom from restriction is a theme of this card. Such moments are fleeting—the Four of Wands invites you to cut loose, enjoy the day, and be jubilant!

Five of Wands

competition ✴ *disagreement*
☾ *teamwork*

Five figures are locked in a tussle—or is it a game? The Five of Wands refers to feeling competitive and taking on your rivals. It can also represent feeling annoyed and having to fight for your rightful place in a group. Maybe a team effort is going wrong, no one is listening and quarrels are surfacing. This card calls on you to engage with disagreements in good spirits. Frustrations are a natural part of teamwork. The question is, what may emerge from the dispute? And what role will you play?

Six of Wands

triumph ☉ *acclaim*
✴ *· flying high*

The Six of Wands is very much a victory card. The battle is over, the contest has been won. A figure rides a horse in a victory procession, wreathed in the laurels that signified glory in Ancient Greece and Rome. This card symbolizes great success in your ventures, particularly the kind of success that follows a long struggle. In a reading, it suggests that you've overcome difficulties and at last your talents are being recognized and praised. It can also warn against arrogance. Bask in the recognition coming your way, but don't let it go to your head.

being assertive ☾ defiance ✴ firmness

speed ✴ motion ☀ conclusion

In life, it can be wise to let things go, and accept a situation. At other times, we must be proactive about sticking up for ourselves. In the Seven of Wands a figure defends themself from challengers. This card invites you to have courage in your convictions and be outspoken. Sometimes asking nicely won't get you anywhere—but expressing yourself firmly and with confidence will. Expect adversity; let your adrenaline energize you. When you confront difficulties head on, it can pay off. Even if it doesn't, you'll know you did your best.

The Eight of Wands is all about accelerating toward a conclusion. You are in the thick of something and life is busy and exciting—a blur that speeds by. Like the wands in the card, events have been catapulted into motion and will fly through the air until they hit the earth with a bump! In a reading, this card evokes the thrill of feeling inspired, being full of energy, and focused on completing a task. It can signify that you are right in the "flow" of a project or phase and encourages you to embrace and use this intensity to your advantage.

Nine of Wands

feeling defensive ☽
pluckiness ✴ *determination*

The man in the Nine of Wands has been through a lot. Covered in bandages, he looks back at the wands resentfully—whilst still being ready for another fight. This card reminds us that arguments take a toll on us. They often leave us feeling touchy and attacked. Yet there can be grace in sticking with the struggle. The Nine of Wands invites you to take stock of your situation and keep seeking resolution if a particular battle really matters to you, even if it causes you discomfort.

Ten of Wands

feeling burdened ✴ *struggle*
☀ *exhaustion*

A figure works to move an armful of wands forward. Though there is a village on the horizon, where they can lay down their burden and recover, the wands obscure their view. This card warns you that the enthusiastic aspect of the Wands suit can lead you into difficulties: maybe you've felt unable to say no to new demands, and then become exhausted. Your energy is spread too thin, and nothing is coming easily. Put aside some responsibilities and reconnect with whatever brings you joy.

PAGE of WANDS.

Page of Wands

eagerness ☾ *learning*
✴ *curiosity*

A youth gazes at the wand in his hands. He is focused, ready to begin a new project. Because this is a Page card—sometimes referred to as the "student" cards—we see the energy of the Wands suit presented in a simple, inexperienced way. This card invites you to start a new project or adventure and be open to learning as you go. Practice makes perfect. In a reading, the Page of Wands may represent you, or someone you know who brings creativity and enthusiasm into a situation.

Knight of Wands

confidence ✴ *charm*
☀ *arrogance*

Though his horse rears up, the knight remains confident and in control. He enjoys the opportunity to show off his skill and bravery. The Knight of Wands brings together the good and the bad of the Wands suit—he is charismatic, athletic, and a conquering hero who wins admiration wherever he goes. He may also be reckless, unreliable, and happy to trample over people's feelings. In a reading, this card might signify that it's time for confidence and action, or it can remind us not to be daunted by people who seem glamorous. We all have strengths, and flaws.

KNIGHT of WANDS.

52

Queen of Wands

confidence ✴ *good fortune*
☾ *encouragement*

Surrounded by sunflowers that represent confidence, the Queen of Wands is a born leader. Relaxed and authoritative, she glows with assurance. Her happiness is infectious—she laughs warmly and brings lightness into any situation. An active and outgoing person, she engages fully with whatever she is doing. Her little black cat symbolizes her mastery of her dark side. This card encourages you to be bold in your endeavors. Picture the Queen of Wands as a friend who sees your potential and says, "all will be well."

QUEEN of WANDS.

KING of WANDS.

King of Wands

self-belief ◉ *skill*
✴ *mentoring*

The King sits alert and upright, looking away from us. The energy of the wands prepares him to use his gifts. He has been through all the stages of creativity: been inspired, taken risks, made mistakes, honed his craft. Now, he is able to do his best work, with great flair. He reminds us that becoming wildly accomplished at something requires determination. As a leader, his success inspires others. In a reading, the King of Wands may represent a mentor, someone who may help you on your journey to become truly skilled at what you love to do.

THE SWORDS

In the tarot, swords represent the power of thought and understanding. They ask, "have you thought about things *like this?*" Just as our minds can solve our problems or cause us to feel stuck, swords can either cut through confusion, or fence us in. As a suit, Swords enlighten us to the pain that truth can bring, as well as the clarity.

Symbolism

Pay close attention to the sky in a Swords card. This is because this suit is paired with the element of air. Is the wind blowing? That wind can represent the turbulence of our thoughts, and their changeable nature. Are there clouds? Dull skies or swirling clouds indicate that clarity is needed.

A sword pointing downwards symbolizes feeling "pinned down" by your thoughts, painfully so. An upright sword suggests a readiness to apply your insights and intellect to a situation. A sword lying flat means a period of reflection. Whatever their position, the Swords suit encourages us to look at the psychology that lies behind our feelings.

Drawing up the Swords

Draw all of the Swords cards from your deck and line them up from Ace through to King. What feelings do the cards prompt in you? The Swords suit is perhaps the most disturbing; you will see despair and disagreement here. Yet these dark moments have lessons to teach us, and among them are moments of illumination.

Ace of Swords

Two of Swords

ACE of SWORDS.

truth—seeking ☾ *a break-through* ✳ *perception*

balance ✳ *tension* ☉ *blocking progress*

A hand grips an upright sword. The blade is crowned and garlanded, and the little droplets around it are a symbol for divinity, suggesting that the sword is blessed from above. The Ace of Swords invites you to begin a quest for a higher level of understanding. Sometimes we forget how powerful our minds can be. This card encourages you to pursue knowledge and truth. Now is the time to start a new project that will stretch your intellect. Revel in discovering new facts!

A blindfolded woman holds up two heavy swords. Dusk falls around her. She is a figure of great stillness and great strength—but where does it leave her? All of her energy is devoted to keeping the swords balanced in a protective cross before her heart. The water flowing behind her symbolizes emotions. She is so focused on keeping her feelings in check, staying guarded, and not taking sides, that she is immobilized. In a reading, this card suggests that it is time to be vulnerable, and to make a decision. That way, you can be free.

Three of Swords

heartache ◗ *sorrow*
✷ *betrayal*

Clouds gather and rain falls behind a love heart, pierced by three swords. Of all the cards, this one cuts deeply in a tender place, and can be painful to look at. The heartache of the Three of Swords may be rooted in a family upset or loss, a falling-out with a friend, or having unrequited feelings for someone. There is a feeling of betrayal—better things were expected than this. In a reading, this card says that it is time to confront painful thoughts. Examine them calmly and remember that one day they will be ancient history.

Four of Swords

rest ✷ *contemplation*
✷ *recovery*

A knight lies entombed in a church. Light filters through a colorful stained-glass window that depicts a woman and child. The knight has retreated from the hurly-burly of battle and lies absolutely still. Sometimes taking a long rest becomes a source of strength. Stepping back from the action also grants us a new perspective on things. The figures in the glass symbolize the life that awaits us when we emerge from a quiet period. This card reminds us of the importance of taking a break, so that we can be refreshed.

disagreement ✳
selfishness ☾ *defeat*

A stormy sky hangs over the afterm_ a dramatic falling-out. The victor_ two upright swords, and one down_ pointing one. He may have won the batt_ what has he lost? His opponents turn_ hunched over and miserable. Perhaps_ need to win is sabotaging your friends_ or perhaps you feel victimized by a comp_ Are you a sore loser—or, even worse, _ winner? This card invites you to set a_ will and remember what really matters._

Six of Swords

feeling low ⊛ *moving on* ✳ *healing*

L ike people seeking refuge from a dangerous place, an adult and child huddle in a small boat. They are being safely guided by a boatman. Yet six swords, symbolic of fears, are plunged into the boat—some of the past is still with them, for now. Will this voyage take them to a safer shore? We do not know—but the duo's escape is underway, and the calm waters ahead suggest peace is in reach. Are you ready to leave a troubling situation behind? The Six of Swords reminds us that it is possible to find hope by moving forward.

Seven of Swords

Eight of Swords

stealth ☾ *independence*
✴ *craftiness*

self-doubt ✴ *helplessness*
☀ *feeling stuck*

A young man with an armful of swords tiptoes away from a gathering. Smiling, he looks to see if someone will stop him. Two swords are left behind, too much for him to manage. Maybe he needs to get away from the group silhouetted on the horizon— or is he tricking them? He may win in the short-term, but will the consequences catch up with him? In a reading, the Seven of Swords could reflect your own actions, or those of someone you know. This card invites the question, is hiding our intentions sensible or selfish?

A figure stands in a watery valley, blindfolded and bound. No help comes. Yet the figure's bonds are loose, and they could free themselves with some effort. Here, the swords symbolize the anxieties that hold us back: fears or unhappy memories. The figure's belief, that they are powerless and in need of rescue, keeps them stuck. When they shrug off their bonds, they will see that the safety of home is close by, on the hill behind them. This card encourages you to move beyond self-doubt and trust in yourself.

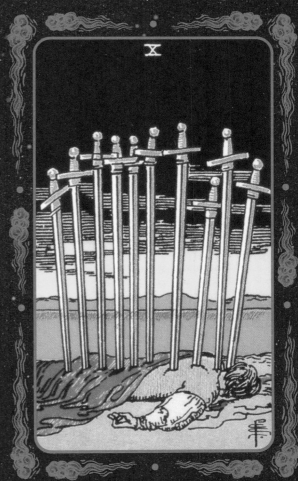

sadness ☾ *despair*
✴ *fearing the worst*

burnout ✴ *drama*
◉ *over-reacting*

The Nine of Swords shows a person troubled by nightmares. This card refers to fears and anxieties that keep us up at night. It is a reminder that experiencing a dark night is universal, and says "you are not alone." Such moments come to us all, and sometimes, we just need to cry. When morning comes, we will feel better, and things will look brighter. In a reading, this card invites you to be gentle with yourself, and to be gentle with others when they go through tough times.

At first glance, this card looks like very bad news. Beneath a black cloud, a man lies pinned by ten swords. But looking closer, we see the sun rising over calm waters. And the number of swords seems unbelievable, a little dramatic. The Ten of Swords shows how distress and exhaustion can lead us to spiral into a dark place. It also hints at how we can relish the drama of being wronged. *Everything is the worst! My life sucks!* If you draw this card in a reading, remember that often things aren't quite as bad as they seem. You'll be okay!

Page of Swords

readiness  *curiosity*
✳ *ignorance*

This young page poses with a sword as clouds sweep across the sky. Pages represent our inner student, and this one is ready to acquire knowledge and cut to the truth of things. A quest is afoot, but this is just a first step: this page has not yet experienced battle, and the cloud by his head suggests that he must address his own ignorance. Experience will dispel this. This card invites you to adopt a humble "beginner's mindset" in order to rise to new challenges.

PAGE of SWORDS.

Knight of Swords

impatience ✳ *conflict*
☀ *enthusiasm*

A knight spurs his horse into battle at full gallop, his sword raised high. This knight is confident with using his intellect to win arguments. He is blessed with certainty and drive. His directness is refreshing. And yet—maybe he likes to debate simply because he likes a fight. Used carelessly, his sword can sever precious bonds. And his opponents may only adopt his view because they *have* to, or just to shut him up! In a reading, his presence raises a question: does confrontation resolve an issue, or make it worse?

KNIGHT of SWORDS.

Queen of Swords

wisdom ✴ *understanding*
☾ *clear thinking*

The Queen of Swords has a solemn expression. She has the kind of authority and wisdom that comes from experience. She has faced trials and come out the other side—transformed. The butterflies on her throne symbolize this transformation. She holds her sword upright, symbolic of justice, and her head is above the clouds. Still, her hand is held out in a gesture of openness. In a reading, she may refer to your own transformation, or to someone you trust to help you with problems, without ever making light of them.

QUEEN of SWORDS.

King of Swords

intellect ☀ *learning*
✴ *action*

The King of Swords has an airy ⟨air⟩ about him. Like the Queen, butt⟨erflies⟩ decorate his throne, and birds fly alo⟨ng⟩ him. He has a cool head, and takes pleas⟨ure in⟩ learning and logic. His face-on stance r⟨eflects⟩ his readiness to confront things. He is ⟨good⟩ at winning debates, values facts highl⟨y, and⟩ is confident with judging right from ⟨wrong.⟩ Warmth may not be his strong suit, ⟨he⟩ reminds us that knowledge is power.

THE PENTACLES

The Pentacles are the practical cards. The pentacles themselves—which appear in some decks as coins—symbolize money. This is the suit where we reflect on resources and security. These cards celebrate the pleasures of getting on with things, and the contentment that achievement brings.

Symbolism

The Pentacles suit is associated with the element of earth. The earth is where we grow food, build homes, and enjoy life. The tarot without this suit would be highly impractical! We need the earthiness of the Pentacles. A reading that is filled with Pentacles cards will explore the rewards of slow, steady effort.

The symbol of roots is important in these cards: roots suggest feeling at home, and being content. Think of earthy metaphors: getting your hands dirty, being down-to-earth, and staying grounded. The star shown on the coins in many decks is called the pentagram. It points downwards, again referring to the need to be rooted in the earth.

Drawing up the Pentacles

Draw all of the Pentacles cards from your deck and line them up from Ace to King. What feelings do these cards prompt in you? This suit contains images of wealth, and poverty too.

Ace of Pentacles

ACE of PENTACLES.

stability ☾ *protection*
✳ *encouragement*

The Ace of Pentacles suggests that a promising time of well-being and security is within reach. If it comes up in a reading, maybe you'll pick up more hours at that part-time job! Bringing together all the power of the Pentacles suit, this golden ace affirms your trustworthy nature, your dedication to doing a good job—and your ability to flourish as you work toward your goals. There is a contrasting feature in this card: follow the little path through the leafy archway and you'll reach the mountains—a reminder that aiming high requires struggle.

Two of Pentacles

focus ✳ *being interested*
◉ *balance*

A dancing figure expertly juggles two pentacles as ships sail the seas behind him. Wholly absorbed, the juggler is not distracted by the wider world. His pentacles move in an infinite figure-of-eight loop, suggesting a smooth flow of energy, a healthy balance. When you pull the Two of Pentacles in a reading, take a moment to think about your pursuits: how are you using your energy? Are you too busy, or bored? It may be time to seek out activities that give you the focused, contented state of mind that the Two of Pentacles embodies.

Three of Pentacles

teamwork  *planning*
✳ *achievement*

Some tasks can be done alone. Others require more thought, more skills, and more time—which means more people. This card is all about the value of teamwork. Three figures work together—each of their voices and skills are equally valuable, and the pressure is shared between them. In a reading, this card could be a sign that it's time to reach out for help and collaborate. Perhaps you have a group project to work on, or a task that's too big to tackle alone.

Four of Pentacles

saving up ✳ *hoarding*
☀ *insecurity*

A man hugs a pentacle-coin close to his chest. His feet pin two pentacles to the ground and a pentacle crowns him. He is focused on hanging on to whatever he already possesses. This card shows how anxiety can rule us, and feed our materialistic tendencies. Just because you "have" something, doesn't mean you'll be happy. Note how this man is immobilized by his need to hang on to what he owns. This card counsels you to value what you have without letting it define you. Make use of it and share it with others—being generous

Five of Pentacles

need ✴ *worry*
☾ *disappointment*

Two unhappy figures trudge through the snow on a dark night. One of them uses crutches and is bandaged up. They need rest, warmth, and care. They walk alongside a lit-up church—but there is no door. Have they been turned away? Or are they so used to surviving on their own that they don't seek help? Though they need a great deal, they have had to learn how to make do with little. In a reading, this card may reflect your own situation or that of people around you. It can act as a nudge to ask for help, or to look out for those who are experiencing hardship.

Six of Pentacles

power ☀ *wealth*
✴ *dependency*

A wealthy merchant gives coins to a beggar, while another waits in hope. Both crouch at his feet. The merchant holds a scale in one hand; he is judging how much to give, and to who. When we lack money, we rely on others to provide—and this can sometimes come with strings attached: *Do this, do that, don't be ungrateful.* This attitude may be one you may find yourself repeating someday, when your own pockets are full! The Six of Pentacles reminds you that when you can, give to others freely, without expecting something in return.

Seven of Pentacles

success 🌙 *taking stock*
✷ *accomplishment*

In this card, each pentacle-coin symbolizes a task. A young man contemplates them before turning to the last task at his feet: he is taking a moment to enjoy the satisfaction that follows hard work. The Seven of Pentacles focuses on how good it feels to look back at a job well done. This card reminds us to celebrate our successes. Next time you are faced with a long list of things to do, find energy by thinking of the satisfaction that will come after you have ticked them all off!

Eight of Pentacles

skill ✷ *focus*
☀ *determination*

A young man bends over his work. All of his energy is focused on getting this particular task done, and done well. The pentacles on the post represent everything he has accomplished so far. The Eight of Pentacles is very similar to the Seven, only here we see someone in full flow. This card is about powering through a big project until it is done or repeating a process until you master it. When you draw this card, think about any projects, tasks, or skills you're working on and remember that focus and practice makes perfect.

Nine of Pentacles

Ten of Pentacles

comfort ☾ *fulfillment*
✳ *plenty*

community ✳ *business-*
as-usual ☉ *exchange*

Agraceful woman walks in a lush garden full of ripe fruit and coins—her life is rich and she has everything needs. A falcon rests on her hand—a sign of her command over her life. A homestead is behind her but she is comfortable where she is. Like the snail at her feet, she is self-sufficient. She has accomplished a great deal, and she is now able to enjoy her prosperity and the independence it gives her. In a reading, this card invites you to take pleasure in your successes. Treat yourself and enjoy the rewards of your efforts—you deserve it!

Abustling marketplace reveals a pair of traders, an elderly man, a playful child, and begging dogs. The Ten of Pentacles celebrates the exchange of goods, money, and wisdom. In some interpretations, the people we see are connected through family ties; in others, they are connected by the bonds of community. This card shows us everyday life when times are good, where the bustle of living alongside others is almost taken for granted. In a reading, you may think of everyday life in your local community, and the traditions you might inherit and choose to observe—or to ignore!

PAGE of PENTACLES.

Page of Pentacles

being studious  *humble*
✳ practical

As with all page cards, this young person is a student, seeking a better understanding of their suit. In the case of the Page of Pentacles, this means learning useful skills and developing a positive approach to work. The figure regards the pentacle-coin with curiosity, focus, and a calm readiness. They know that patience and effort will be required for them to become successful. The next time you sit down to tackle an assignment that doesn't thrill you, let this page serve as a gentle inspiration to you.

Knight of Pentacles

predictable ✳ steady
✳ reliable

Of all the knights, the Knight of Pentacles is the least flashy. He keeps watch, and his stillness is matched by both his horse and the land he surveys. More of a guardian than a warrior, he can be depended upon. In fact, he is so reliable, he can be a little bit dull. He doesn't care if he or his ways bore you—he cares about doing things well. In a reading, this knight may represent a person in your life, or he may relate to your own approach to a task. Half of the battle is showing up—and the rest is sticking with it.

KNIGHT of PENTACLES.

Queen of Pentacles

resourceful ✦ *down-to-earth* ☾ *nurturing* ·

The Queen of Pentacles sits in a sunlit valley. Vines and fruit grow all about her throne, creating a haven filled with the gentle wealth of fall. The rabbit playing nearby symbolizes the energy of new life. This queen knows how to cultivate possibilities—she can make any plant grow, and any flower bloom. Being part of the Pentacles, she has a practical nature. She is steady, insightful, and takes things in her stride. In a reading, she reminds us that our abilities can be a source of deep contentment.

QUEEN of PENTACLES.

KING of PENTACLES.

King of Pentacles

hands-on ✺ *capable* ✦ *prosperous*

The King of Pentacles' robes are decorated with fruit and golden leaves that echo the gold of the sky and the plants around his throne. He is almost part of the landscape—fittingly so, because this king is all about getting his hands dirty. Highly skilled, he enjoys learning by doing. His presence in a reading often relates to business and making money. When it comes to being successful, he would advise you to make use of your natural abilities.

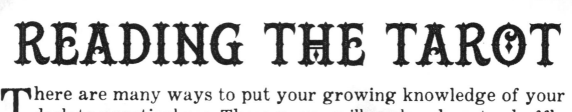

READING THE TAROT

There are many ways to put your growing knowledge of your deck to practical use. These pages will explore how to shuffle your deck, how to do readings—for yourself and for others—and will give examples of a few different spreads you can try.

HOW TO READ TAROT

There are many ways to read tarot. You can use it as a tool for introspection—guiding you in your own decisions and quandaries. You can also use it to help others do the same.

Whether you're reading for yourself or for another querent, here are some steps and guides you can follow:

1. Choose a comfy, quiet spot where you are unlikely to be interrupted.

2. Make sure you or the querent shuffle the deck before each reading.

3. Spread the cards in a line, face down. Then draw out the number of cards you need at random, one-by-one, keeping them face down until you're ready to begin. If you're reading for another querent, have them draw the cards.

4. Don't rush. Turn over only one card at a time. Give yourself or the querent time to respond to it and the emotions it produces before moving on to the next card in the spread.

5. If it is a three- (or more) card reading, take a moment to reflect on the whole of what you see once all of the cards face up. Are they mostly bright colors or dark ones? Are there several from one suit, or a mix? What are your overall observations? If you're reading for a querent, ask for their observations, and share your own thoughts with them, too.

TIPS FOR READING FOR YOURSELF

✳ Let go of expectations

Come to the cards with curiosity. Reading your tarot immediately after something has happened, such as an argument or a break-up, will not yield much wisdom. Wait until you feel calmer and able to listen to what the cards show you.

☽ Give yourself time

Once you've asked the cards about a particular situation, give yourself time to work through what the reading meant. Set an intention based on what you learned, and act on it. You can always revisit your dilemma again, but see what shifts first. Aim to leave at least a week between repeat readings so that your new insights can emerge.

❂ Create a ritual

Many tarot practitioners follow a simple routine that helps them prepare for a reading. Lighting some incense, meditating, making a soothing drink, or playing mood-setting music are good ways to move into a more reflective frame of mind.

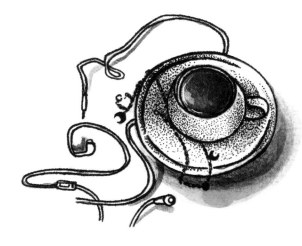

☽ Keep a journal

Making notes on a tarot reading can make it more powerful. For each reading, write down or sketch out the cards, their positions, and your responses to them in a journal. Looking back at past readings will help you gain confidence in your ability to read for yourself.

TIPS FOR READING FOR OTHERS

✳ Listen without advising

The key to becoming a good tarot reader is to listen. In a reading, it's important to remember you are not there to give advice—you are there to help another person interpret the cards, and so understand their own situation more deeply. You can help them gain insight through a reading—*but what they do next is entirely up to them.*

☾ Have the right intentions

In the wrong hands, tarot can be used to upset a querent, or persuade them to reveal private things they regret sharing. This abuses the power of the cards. Anyone who uses tarot to hurt someone, rather than help them, should be avoided!

⊙ Keep it confidential

What is said in the tarot reading, stays in the tarot reading! Trust is key—if you tell everyone about what someone shared with you in a reading, you break that trust.

☾ Look after yourself

Doing many readings means you will listen to many people's problems. This can leave you feeling drained. It's okay to say no to friends who want readings, if you are not feeling up to it! Keep some of your care and wisdom back for yourself, so that you may continue on your tarot journey with a clear head, and a full heart.

INTERPRETING THE CARDS

How you interpret tarot cards is down to you. There's no wrong way! What's important is how the cards make you feel and what questions and answers they prompt in you. Here's a little guidance to get you started...

When you pull a card, spend time reacting to it before you look up its meaning. Examine your own reactions to the colors, symbols, and figures. *How does the card make you feel? What does it remind you of?* If you're reading for another querent, ask them these questions and let them discuss them with you and react to them as much as they wish to.

When you're ready, read the card's meaning in this book and re-examine your feelings and interpretations. You can use the key words next to the card meanings for a snapshot of each card's associated energy, and you can turn to the symbols and meanings section (see pages 22–24) to learn more about the imagery.

For each card, consider the following:

What kind of card is it? Major Arcana cards often relate to big life events, while Minor Arcana cards relate to day-to-day issues.

What suit is it? Pentacles cards could suggest issues around home or money, while Cups cards could relate to love and relationships.

Does the card's meaning or energy remind you of a person or situation in your life?

Could the card represent something you'd like to embody, or something you need to let go?

What is the card inviting you to do, or ask? For example, The Hanged Man could prompt you to be patient, while the Five of Swords might guide you to question your actions.

At the end of a reading, pay attention to how you (or your querent) feel. Sometimes you may draw cards that seem disconnected with the question or problem you're working with—and this is okay! A baffling card may suggest that the issue it represents is not "live" for you right now. And if your own feelings about a card don't tally with the meaning in the book, this is okay, too. The descriptions are there to prompt and inspire—you can always follow your own intuition.

Remember, no matter what the cards show you, what happens next is within your power.

THE DAILY CARD PULL

A very popular use of tarot cards is to pull a single card each day, usually in the morning, to draw on the wisdom of tarot in daily life. This method of reading tarot is also a great way to become truly familiar with each and every card.

How to do a daily card pull:

1. Settle yourself somewhere quiet and shuffle your deck. When you feel ready, spread the cards in an arc before you. Ask yourself, "what message do I need to hear today?"

2. Draw one card out. Turn it over. How does the image make you feel? You first reaction is part of getting to know your deck, and part of reading tarot.

3. Look up your card in this book. How do you feel about the card now? What does it remind you of, today?

4. Think about what the card *and your response to it* has taught you. Perhaps write about the card in your journal. Allow your thoughts to return to the meanings and the images throughout the day.

The daily card pull allows you to learn about each card deeply and steadily. Don't worry if you miss a few days or can't remember the meanings for a card you have pulled before— keep going, and over time, you will develop a rich store of associations to return to!

THE THREE-CARD SPREAD

A single tarot card tells you something about one particular moment, mood, or situation. It's practical, but it can be limiting. When you put tarot cards together in a spread, you will find a whole story that shines a light on your situation.

A THREE-CARD SPREAD is perfect for when you, or your querent, are feeling a bit stuck on an everyday problem. The cards can refresh your thinking and reveal a path forward. There are many ways of doing a three-card reading.

Before you start, decide on a question or problem, then choose a structure for your reading. Here are some example structures:

THE PAST (card 1), THE PRESENT (card 2), THE FUTURE (card 3)

AN ISSUE (card 1), THE CAUSE (card 2), THE SOLUTION (card 3)

YOU (card 1), ANOTHER PERSON (card 2), WHAT MAY HAPPEN (card 3)

GOAL (card 1), OBSTACLE (card 2), ACTION (card 3)

When you're ready, shuffle and draw your cards, interpreting them one at a time. How does each card make you feel? How does each card relate to the structure of the spread? This may not always be clear straight away, so dig deep. Say you draw a card that symbolizes the past—does it remind you of someone or something from recent months? Did you once embody the energy of this card? Or perhaps it is the opposite—does the card point to what was *missing* from your past? Look for what resonates with you.

When all three cards are facing up, what story do you feel they tell? And what will you do now?

THE CELTIC CROSS SPREAD

T his ten-card spread is perfect for when you want to try an in-depth tarot reading, either for yourself or for others. Use it to dig deeply into a more specific dilemma, for example: *"What should I do about [a particular situation]?"*

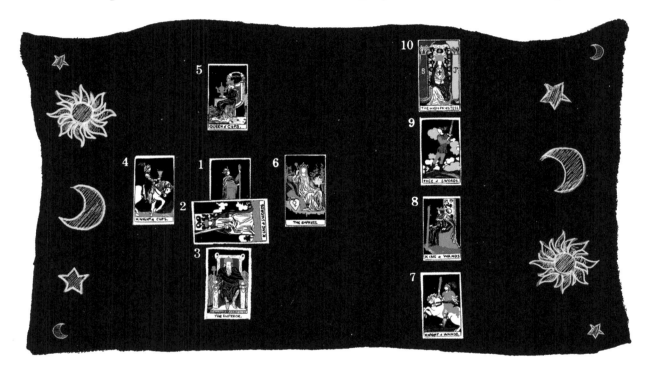

Key:

1. That Which Covers You – you and your situation
2. That Which Crosses You – an obstacle blocking your path
3. A Conscious Thought – something on your mind; a known factor
4. The Past – a circumstance that brought you here
5. Root Cause – the unexplored foundation of your dilemma
6. The Future – new circumstances that will emerge
7. You & Your Role – your current state of mind
8. That Which Surrounds You – your environment, i.e. the people around you, and where you spend your time
9. Hopes & Fears – can also be Hopes OR Fears
10. Outcome – where your situation may take you

Shuffle the cards as you ponder your dilemma. If you're reading for someone else, encourage your querent to shuffle and talk through their dilemma with you.

Take the cards and fan them out face-down, then draw, or ask the querent to draw, out ten cards. Once ten cards have been drawn, you can arrange them into the layout shown opposite.

When ready to start, turn over the card in the no. 1 position, and, if you're reading for someone else, explain the card to your querent. Ask them for their thoughts and listen to their answer. If you're reading for yourself, examine your own thoughts and feelings in response to each card.

As with the three-card spread, consider each card in relation to its position. Examine your first reaction, look up the card's meaning, and think about where it has appeared in the spread. Then make an interpretation about how it connects to your situation.

Repeat the process until all ten cards are visible. Consider the story that the cards are telling. How do you or your querent feel about it? A full celtic cross spread can take up to one hour to read.

BEYOND THE BOOK

You have started on a journey of discovery, truth-seeker—
and though this book ends here, the journey goes on. You are
now equipped with knowledge that will serve you well as you
explore tarot for yourself and with others. Seek out those
who share your curiosity, and learn from each other as you
become practiced in the art of reading these precious cards.

Knowing what you now know about tarot can bring you
clarity, insight, and wisdom throughout your life. As you
experience all that living can offer, from love to loss and
everything in between, remember that the cards will always
be there, ready for whenever you need them.